Shopkins™
Once you shop...You can't stop!

WELCOME TO SHOPVILLE!
By Jenne Simon

Published by Scholastic Inc., *Publishers since 1920.* SCHOLASTIC and associated logos are trademarks and/or registered trademarks of Scholastic Inc.

The publisher does not have any control over and does not assume any responsibility for author or third-party websites or their content.

ISBN 978-0-545-91295-2

10 9 8 7 6 5 4 3 2   15 16 17 18 19

Printed in the U.S.A.   40

This edition first printing, September 2015   •   Book design by Erin McMahon

Scholastic Inc.

Welcome to Shopville, the home of the Shopkins™! Apple Blossom, Cheeky Chocolate, and all their friends love to hang out at Small Mart. And today, they're competing in the Shopville Games. Check it out!

THE SHOPVILLE GAMES!

3

Once a year, the Shopkins show off their sporting skills during the Shopville Games! Here are this year's attendees:

Apple Blossom is juiced up and ready to go.

Cheeky Chocolate never breaks under pressure!

Spilt Milk will cream last year's records.

Lippy Lips has colorful cheers to encourage her friends!

Kooky Cookie doesn't crumble when the chips are down.

And Strawberry Kiss always gives her berry best!

The first event is the Shopping Cart Sprint. Spilt Milk wants to beat the record for the fastest dash down the aisle. "I'm feeling fresh and ready to race!" she says.

On your mark, get set, go! Apple Blossom and Cheeky Chocolate push Spilt Milk's cart down the aisle.

"Faster! I need to go faster!" cries Spilt Milk. "Team, I can taste victory, but I need your help!"

Spilt Milk's race crew won't let her down! But can they make it across the finish line fast enough?

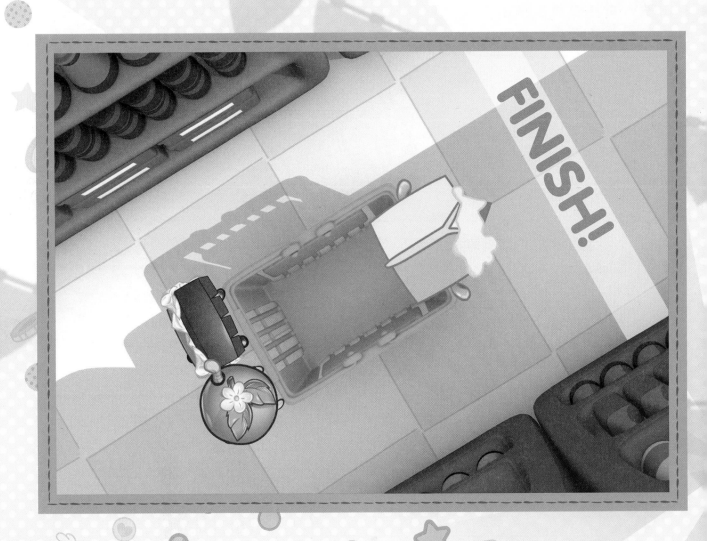

8

Yes, they can! Spilt Milk has beaten the record and soaks up the applause.

"You're spoiling me!" she says. "I could never have done it without my friends."

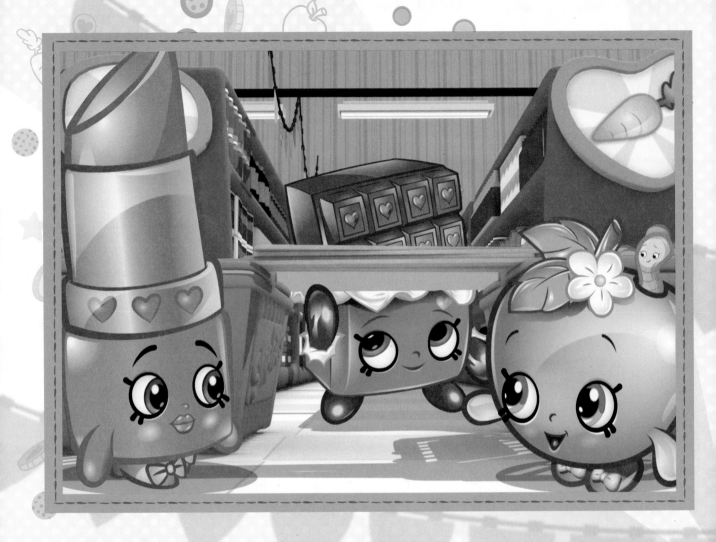

The next event is the Popsicle Stick Chop. Cheeky Chocolate is nervous. "I've only ever broken through two sticks before," she says. "But this year I'm trying for three!"

"You can lick those sticks!" Lippy Lips cheers.

Cheeky is ready. She thinks sweet thoughts, jumps high in the air, and does her signature chocolate chop!
"HI-YA!"

CRACK! All three sticks splinter right down the middle. "You've broken your own record!" cries Apple Blossom. Cheeky couldn't be happier. "Isn't life sweet?"

Next up is the Frozen Food Climb. Apple Blossom, Strawberry Kiss, and Cheeky Chocolate all race to see who can reach the top of Frozen Food Mountain in record time.

Climbing Frozen Food Mountain is hard work!
"If I weren't so cold, I'd probably melt!" groans Cheeky.

But Apple Blossom still has some juice left. With a burst of speed, she reaches the top and breaks the record!
"Deep down in my core, I always knew I had it in me!" she says.

The Checkout Jump is the final event. It's the toughest competition yet. Shopkins will be judged on the skill of their jumps over the checkout scanner . . . and their style!

Kooky Cookie is the favorite to win.

"She'll be one tough cookie to beat," says Apple Blossom.

CHECKOUT JUMP!

17

FLIP!

But are they made
of the right stuff to win?

19

It's Kooky Cookie's turn. She gets a running start and soars into the air to swing from the banners. Round and round she goes, bigger and faster than anyone has before!

Suddenly, the banner breaks!
"Oh, no! My big flip is going to be a big *floooooop!*" cries Kooky.

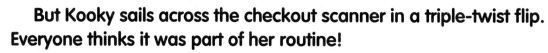

But Kooky sails across the checkout scanner in a triple-twist flip. Everyone thinks it was part of her routine!

"That jump was just delicious!" Apple says.

"And it was a record breaker—you got the sweetest score ever for creativity!" says Cheeky.

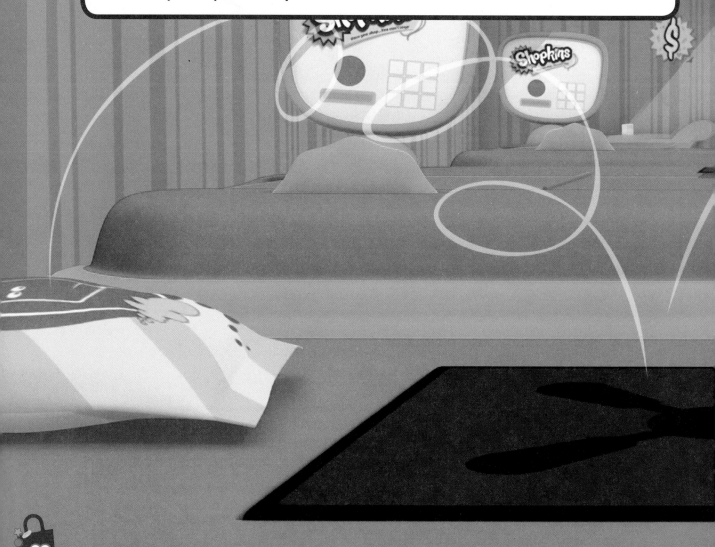

The Shopville Games have been a huge success!
Because when you have friends like the Shopkins, everyone wins!